THE ACROBAT & THE ANGEL

MARK SHANNON

ILLUSTRATED BY DAVID SHANNON

G. P. PUTNAM'S SONS • NEW YORK

For my family —M. S.

To Heidi and Emma, my angels —D. S.

Péquelé is pronounced PAY-kul-lay

"The Acrobat of God (or of Our Lady)" is a French folktale from the twelfth or thirteenth century. I found Péquelé's name in a charming version collected by Henri Pourrat (*French Folktales*. New York: Pantheon, 1989). In developing the story for children, I have tried to integrate historical details and to bring forward a popular appeal that transcends strict religious orthodoxy, an appeal intrinsic to the tale since its beginning. Also, the plague introduced here is not meant to refer to the Black Death of 1347-1350. Finally, I hope this version keeps our acrobat's spirit as alive and engaging as ever. —M. S.

The art was done in acrylic on illustration board.

Once there was a poor lad named Péquelé. When Péquelé was still just a baby, the plague had struck his village and both his parents fell desperately ill. They sent Péquelé away with his grandmother to the other side of the mountains. That was the last Péquelé saw of his mother or father. But into Péquelé's blanket his mother had tucked an angel she had made of branches and dried flowers.

From the time he could walk, Péquelé showed a love for leaps and somersaults. By the time he was seven, he would get dressed every morning, and then walk from his grandmother's stone cottage to the square in the village nearby. First he would juggle with wooden balls. Then he would leap into the air like a fish, and then tumble across the cobblestones, twisting his limbs into the craziest shapes. By the time he was nine, he could bound to the edge of the square's fountain and race around the rim on his hands. Péquelé was an acrobat. His grandmother made him some special clothes, and day after day he put all the joy he had into his tricks. Little children especially loved Péquelé.

"Hooray for Péquelé!" the crowds would say.

A few coins would plunk into Péquelé's hat. By nightfall, the money he'd gathered would buy just enough food for him and his grandmother.

Every night before dinner, Péquelé and his grandmother would kneel down to pray before the angel Péquelé's mother had left them. They would give thanks for each other and, as Péquelé's grandmother would say, "for the warmth and light inside us, which is all simple folks like ourselves can understand of God's mysterious ways."

But one autumn morning, Péquelé awoke to find his grandmother's body without life. Her soul had passed on without warning.

Alone and with nothing to eat, Péquelé left his home. He was too sad to perform his tricks. Instead he wandered, begging scraps of food. As he went along, he heard that another outbreak of the plague had struck the villages on the other side of the mountains. Everyone said God was angry with all the sin in the world. People were more frightened than ever of misfortune. They wanted nothing to do with Péquelé. He slept in stables with the horses, and then wandered on.

Finally, one bitterly cold December evening, he collapsed
on the steps of a roadside cross.

As he lay silent and still, it began to snow.

Late the next afternoon, Péquelé slowly opened his eyes. A man sitting next to him smiled through the steam of a bowl of broth he held. "Thank God we have not lost you. My name is Friar John," the man said. He told Péquelé he had come across him on his way back from the village. "Now, let us get you something to eat," Friar John concluded, and he helped Péquelé out of bed.

Friar John took Péquelé to a kitchen, where the two of them sat in front of a roaring, crackling fire and talked while Friar John gave Péquelé his fill of a bean-and-sausage stew. As Péquelé revived, he told Friar John about his grandmother and his life as an acrobat, and about the prayers and the angel that always inspired him.

"I am sure your grandmother and your parents are watching over you from heaven, Péquelé," Friar John replied. "We have a statue of an angel in our cloister. Would you like to see it?"

Péquelé nodded.

Friar John took Péquelé to the back of a chapel.
When Péquelé saw the statue, his limbs started to tingle.
Memories of home and of his mother's angel flooded his
heart. He couldn't help but crouch and leap into the air,
bursting into a series of handsprings and back flips
around the chapel, his eyes shining.

Suddenly heavy footsteps sounded at the doorway.

"John!" came a commanding voice. Péquelé stopped. A man marched down the drafty length of the chapel, then whispered with Friar John. Finally Friar John introduced Péquelé to the Abbot, the head of the monastery.

"My poor son," began the Abbot, "our chapel is a place of calm prayer and worship. It is no place for a circus. You may take shelter here only if you leave your carnival ways behind forever. Do I have your promise?"

Péquelé reached out and touched the robe of the angel. "I promise," he said.

Péquelé took a room next to Friar John's, and the man and the boy became like father and son. They ate their meals side by side, flanked by the other friars at the monastery's long table. The friars enjoyed Péquelé's sweet nature, but the Abbot kept a stern eye on his behavior.

Each day Péquelé would do the different chores Friar John found
for him, and every night he went to the angel and prayed, just as he
always had. He missed his grandmother, but the angel's presence
brought him comfort, and Péquelé gave thanks for his new home.

One spring afternoon, after Friar John had gone to pick up supplies in the village, Péquelé was sweeping the monastery's front steps when he heard a child crying. Before long a woman approached, cradling a small, wailing boy in her arms.

"Oh, please, Friar," she pleaded, "won't you bless my baby? I fear for his life."

Péquelé turned to look behind him, to see who the woman was addressing. But no one else was there. When he looked again at the child, he saw the black splotches. The little boy had caught the plague. Péquelé gasped, unsure what to do.

"Please, Friar, I have journeyed far to come here. I beg you," cried the woman.

So Péquelé put aside the broom. He made a butterfly with his hands. The child's wild blue eyes turned toward Péquelé's graceful fingers, which began to fly and flit about the steps as though they had a mind of their own, with the rest of Péquelé trying to keep up.

The boy waved his small arms, and his crying subsided. Péquelé's butterfly flew closer. Suddenly the child burst into a wail again. His hot, pained breath struck Péquelé's face.

Péquelé could not bear the child's suffering. He paused and glanced around quickly, remembering his promise to the Abbot.

Then Péquelé sprang into his tricks. He gave the child all the joy he shared with the crowds in the square not long ago. He jumped onto his hands and walked on them like a funny creature up the steps. The child stopped crying. Then Péquelé launched himself from the top step and turned two somersaults in the air. But just as the child's laughter rang out, the Abbot's looming figure appeared in the doorway behind Péquelé. His eyes were flashing with anger.

"Péquelé!" the Abbot shouted. "You have broken your promise." Then he looked at the woman and her child. "God forgive us. This child carries the plague. And now perhaps *you* have caught the disease as well," he said, pointing at Péquelé. "You have betrayed us all before God. You must leave at once!" With that, he went back into the monastery and slammed the heavy, carved doors behind him.

Péquelé stood in shock.

Just then Friar John returned from his errands, hurrying beneath the light afternoon rain. He listened to Péquelé recount what had happened.

Friar John spoke urgently to the woman. "Don't go back to your village. Wait for us at the cross near the bottom of the hill. We will come for you soon."

"Friar John, may I see the angel one last time?" Péquelé's face was pale, and his eyes were welling with tears.

"Of course, Péquelé," Friar John said. "Of course. But we must hurry."

♦ ♦ ♦

"Angel," Péquelé said, "if I must leave you, I thank you with all that I have for all the warmth and light you have given me. Please, bless the friars and the poor woman and her little boy."

Then Péquelé leapt into the air. Friar John had never seen such tricks performed with so much spirit, so much soul.

It was like a beautiful, hypnotizing dance.

Nevertheless, he began to move forward to stop Péquelé.

But at that very moment the chapel
began filling with light. As Friar John watched
with eyes wide in astonishment, the statue began to stir. The angel
lifted her wings and glided toward Péquelé on a ray of gleaming
white light. She took Péquelé's hand, and the two of them began
to float off the ground together, slowly rising until they became
a single figure, which then vanished into the air.

"Heaven be upon us," said a voice behind Friar John. "What have I done?"

Friar John turned to see the Abbot holding his cross over his heart.

When Friar John turned around again, he saw white petals falling like snow from heaven. He remembered finding Péquelé that cold December evening.

As his memory drifted through all his days with Péquelé, Friar John watched the petals turn into white butterflies. And then these too were gone.

Friar John went again to the roadside cross, where he found the woman holding her child. The child's skin was bright and clear. Péquelé had vanished, but so had all traces of the plague. In fact, the plague never came again to the villages around the monastery, and the next fall's harvest was bountiful.

Friar John and the Abbot knew they had witnessed a miracle that day.

So, in the place where the angel's statue once stood, there now rests a statue of Péquelé—the Acrobat of God. And if you were ever to visit the monastery, you just might see a friar or two out in the orchard . . .

. . . turning a somersault in the sweet spring air.